Diary of a BABY Wombat

by Jackie French

illustrated by
Bruce Whatley

 Clarion Books • Houghton Mifflin Harcourt • Boston / New York • 2010

*To Lisa, who has crafted the journey of Bruce, Mothball, and me
from the beginning, and added endless magic.
P.S. And to Noël, Jennifer, Bounce, and Burper too, with much love.
J.F.*

*For Sylvia Rose
B.W.*

Clarion Books
215 Park Avenue South
New York, New York 10003

Text copyright © 2009, 2010 by Jackie French
Illustrations copyright © 2009 by Farmhouse Illustration Company Pty Limited

First published as *Baby Wombat's Week* in Australia in 2009 by Angus & Robertson,
an imprint of Harper Collins Publishers, Australia. Published in the United States in 2010.

For information about permission to reproduce selections from this book,
write to Permissions, Houghton Mifflin Harcourt Publishing Company,
215 Park Avenue South, New York, New York 10003.

www.hmhbooks.com

The illustrations were executed in acrylic paints on watercolor paper.
The text was set in Kid's Stuff Plain.

Clarion Books is an imprint of Houghton Mifflin Harcourt Publishing Company.

Library of Congress Cataloging-in-Publication Data

French, Jackie.
 Diary of a baby wombat / written by Jackie French ; illustrated by Bruce Whatley.
   p. cm.
 Summary: Through a week of diary entries, a wombat describes his life of sleeping, playing,
and helping his mother look for a bigger hole in which to make their home.
 ISBN 978-0-547-43005-8
1. Wombats—Juvenile fiction. [1. Wombats—Fiction. 2. Diaries—Fiction.] I. Whatley, Bruce, ill. II. Title.

PZ10.3.F8855Dhb 2010
[E]—dc22
2009050452

Manufactured in China

China 10 9 8 7 6 5 4 3 2 1

4500230556

I'm a wombat. So is my mum.

We live in Australia.

We eat mainly grass — and a few treats.

Our home is a hole in the ground.

My mum sleeps there during the day.

So do I . . . some of the time.

Monday

Early morning: Slept.

Slept.

Late morning: Slept.

Woke up.

Bounced.

Mum decided
it was time to PLAY . . .

OUTSIDE!

Smelled the flowers.

Ate the flowers.

A new smell! Where . . . ?

Here it is!

Someone to play with!

Afternoon: Played.

I won!

Tuesday

Early morning: Slept.

Slept.

Late morning: Played.

Later morning: Ate.

Afternoon: Slept.

Wednesday

Morning: Woke up.

BORED...

Mum says we need more room. A BIGGER hole!

Dug a new hole.

Afternoon:
Scratched.

Thursday

Morning: Mum says new hole is too small.

Afternoon: Hunted for **another** new hole.

All the holes are too small.

Will we **ever** find a hole **BIG** enough for Mum and me?

Friday

Morning:

Found a GIANT hole!

Afternoon:
Told Mum about hole!

Mum said, "Go to sleep."

Saturday

Morning: Someone stole our hole!

Mum says never mind.

We'll dig the BEST hole EVER!

Night:

We're digging a
special kind of hole . . .

a tunnel!

What's up there?

We've found the most ENORMOUS hole!

Big enough for me . . . and my mum.

And everyone.

Sunday

Morning: Slept.